Noah Builds an Ark

Noah Builds an Ark

Kate Banks

illustrated by John Rocco

CANDLEWICK PRESS

Noah spied it coming from afar. It started with a cloud peeping over the hill like a curious ghost. A storm was on the way.

Noah watched the salamanders slither to and fro restlessly in the garden. The beetles burrowed deeper into their bed of bark. The gray field mice stuffed a hole in a log with a cushion of moss to shelter themselves. And the ants played tug-of-war with a dried twig.

"It's going to be a beauty," said Noah's father as he came down into the backyard. "We'd better get ready."

He went to fetch some wood and his tools.

"We need to get ready, too," said Noah to the creatures in the garden. And he went to fetch his wagon.

Noah's father began to board up the windows. Noah set to work
with his own tools.

And while a grasshopper looked on knowingly, Noah built an ark.

"Better be prepared," said Noah's mother from the kitchen.

She and Noah's sister were stacking groceries in the cupboards
and filling jugs of water for the coming days.

"Better be prepared," whispered Noah to the creatures in the garden.

And he gathered food for the ark: fists of brown nuts, spears of grass, berries, and seeds.

Noah's mother got out the candles
and matches. "There's no knowing
in a storm," she said.

"No knowing," repeated Noah to
the grasshopper. And he wedged
a small flashlight into the bow of
the ark. Then he furnished the ark
with a miniature table and chairs,
some tiny cups and saucers, and
a small bed.

"Come," called Noah's mother.

"Come," whispered Noah to the creatures in the garden.

The salamanders slid shyly from beneath the rock wall,

the spotted toads leaped from under a large silvery leaf,

and the grass snakes slithered from around a tree stump.

The little gray field mice peeked out from their hollow log,

the beetles and the spiders scurried as fast as their legs would take them,

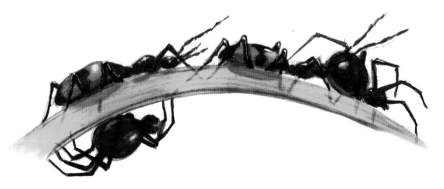

and the hummingbird in the rosebush fluttered her wings.

Into the ark all the creatures went, two by two.
"I will come get you when the storm has passed,"
said Noah, closing the door.

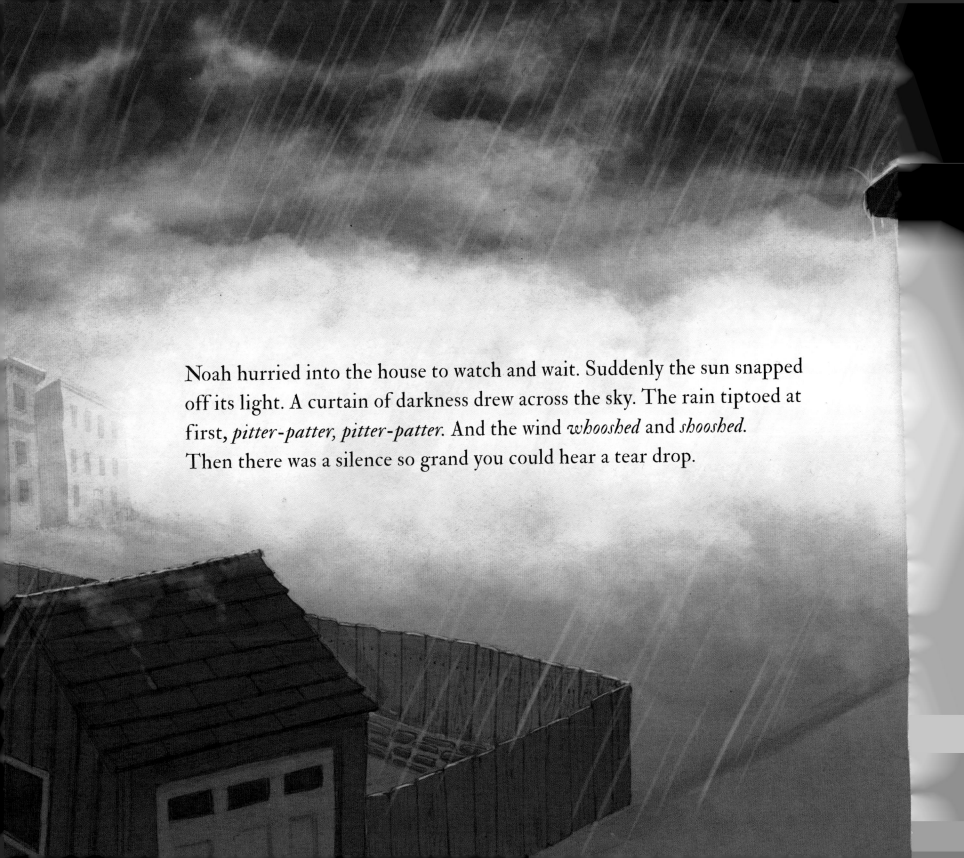

Noah hurried into the house to watch and wait. Suddenly the sun snapped off its light. A curtain of darkness drew across the sky. The rain tiptoed at first, *pitter-patter, pitter-patter*. And the wind *whooshed* and *shooshed*. Then there was a silence so grand you could hear a tear drop.

Pretty soon the wind began to roar, banging at the door and on the walls of the house. *Let me come in,* it seemed to say.

The rain splashed down like silver swords thrown from heaven. Noah huddled on the couch next to his little sister and Boots, the cat.

Inside the ark, the creatures clustered around the tiny table in a tight circle.

Noah's mother made sandwiches and lemonade. And they played a board game by candlelight.

Inside the ark, the creatures nibbled on nuts and seeds. The toads hopped across the mice's tails. And the spider wove pretty pictures on the wall.

When evening came, Noah's father sat down in the rocking chair and told stories to drown out the pelting rain and the howling wind.

Inside the ark, the snake hissed and the beetles click-clacked. Each little creature made a noise of its own. *Squeak, squawk, tick-tock, knock-knock.*

Then Noah's mother sang until Noah's eyes grew heavy, and he climbed the stairs to bed.

In the ark, the crickets chirped and the hummingbird hummed. And in no time at all, the world — except for the storm — was asleep.

For four days and nights, the storm raged. Raindrops swelled into puddles, then small ponds. The water rose up and up until the ark appeared to float across the garden in a sea of debris. Noah watched it anxiously as he peeked from the upstairs window.

But suddenly the wind changed direction.

The heavens closed, and as suddenly as it had started,
the rain stopped and the water began to recede.

The clouds retreated, and the sun turned its light back on.

Above, a rainbow stretched across the sky.
"Hallelujah," said Noah's father.
"Hallelujah," said Noah.

That afternoon, Noah's father took the boards down from
the windows, and Noah opened the door of the ark wide.
"Come out, come out," he cried.
The creatures exited the ark two by two.

And once again the garden was swarming with life.

For Oliver — K. B.

To Laurel Adam (aka Marme) — J. R.

First edition 2019

Library of Congress Catalog Card Number pending
ISBN 978-0-7636-7484-7

18 19 20 21 22 23 TLF 10 9 8 7 6 5 4 3 2 1

Printed in Dongguan, Guangdong, China

This book was typeset in IM FELL Double Pica.
The illustrations were done in pencil and watercolor and rendered digitally.

Candlewick Press
99 Dover Street
Somerville, Massachusetts 02144

visit us at www.candlewick.com